BAD FOOD

Mission Impastable

By Eric Luper

Illustrated by
"The Doodle Boy" Joe Whale

Scholastic Inc.

All rights reserved. Published by Scholastic Inc., *Publishers since 1920.* SCHOLASTIC and associated logos are trademarks and/or registered trademarks of Scholastic Inc.

The publisher does not have any control over and does not assume any responsibility for author or third-party websites or their content.

ISBN 978-1-338-83542-7

2 2022

Printed in the U.S.A.   23

First printing 2022

Book design by Katie Fitch

SCHOOL MAP

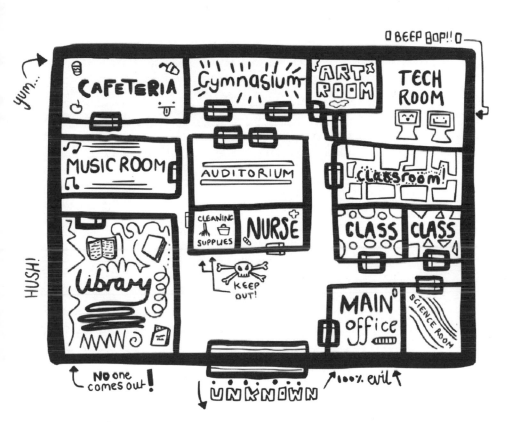

CHAPTER 1

Noodling Around

Once again, night came to Belching Walrus Elementary. The doors were locked, the hallways were silent, and the air-conditioning lazily puffed out cool air. Oh, and all the food in the cafeteria was chilling out.

No, what I meant to say is that the food in the cafeteria at Belching Walrus Elementary actually comes alive each night to hang out and have fun. Every night.

And ever since the folks from the other rooms in the school helped Slice, Scoop, and Totz stop the sneaky plans of the aliens, Gleb and Lauren . . .

Well, it's all been pretty good since then.

And, as always, best buds Slice (a brave triangular slice of pizza), Scoop (a triple scoop ice cream cone—vanilla, chocolate, AND strawberry), and Totz (a crunchy, delicious, and trendy tater tot) were doing a little bit of their own chilling out under the utility sink.

"So, what have you guys been up to?" Slice asked.

"Not a lot," Totz said. "Now that I've mastered the

art of the cartwheel, I'm back to writing my rhymes. Oh, and learning how to play the banjo."

"Can you play a song for us?" Scoop asked.

"Nah," Totz said. "I'm not good enough yet."

"Oh, come on," Slice said. "I'm sure it'll be great."

Totz plucked a few strings and then shook his head. "Not yet," he said. "How about you, Scoop?"

"Me? I've been working hard at going legit."

"Legit?" Slice said. "What does that mean?"

Scoop turned around a small piece of canvas. On it, she had painted a beautiful picture of the word *zap* in bubble letters surrounded by all sorts of sparkly shapes and colors.

"I've started using glitter in my art," Scoop said. "And I paint on canvas now. I got it from the Art Room."

"I like when you paint on the walls," Slice said.

"Yeah," added Totz. "They are so big and eye-catching."

"The cleaning supplies complained about the mess," Scoop explained. "So, I started creating my art on canvas. I can give them as gifts."

She handed one to Totz and another to Slice. "These are for you."

"Thanks!" Totz and Slice both said at once.

"I know just where I'm going to hang it," Totz said.

"Me too," Slice said. "But, Scoop, you have to sign it. All famous artists sign their paintings."

"Yeah," Totz added. "Right down there in the corner."

Scoop's strawberry ice cream flushed a little pinker, but she dipped a finger in her chocolate scoop and signed her name along the bottom edge.

"Glizzy and Sprinkles want me to do an art show," she said. "They hung my paintings in the hallway, but I'm not so sure."

In case you were not paying attention in the first two adventures, or in case you didn't know this was the third book in the series and you are new to Belching Walrus Elementary, or in case you completely forgot, let's get to know a few of our characters . . .

Glizzy

Name: Glizzy

Food Type: Hot dog

Personality: Wise and gruff

Strengths: A born leader, knows a lot from the old days

Weaknesses: Can't go outside—it's too much to bear after becoming a leftover at the Great School Cookout!

Fear: Soggy irritable bowel syndrome, or SBS (if you think you may suffer from SBS, talk to your doctor or pharmacist)

Is a hot dog a sandwich?: A hot dog is *more* than just a sandwich.

Sprinkles

Name: Sprinkles

Food Type: Pink frosted donut with sprinkles

Personality: Sweet and kind

Strengths: Brings folks together

Weaknesses: Worries often and loses a lot of sprinkles

Hobbies: Knitting sweaters anyway (does food need a sweater?)

"Why wouldn't you want to do an art show?" Slice asked.

Scoop shrugged. "What if people don't like it? What if they laugh at me? It's one thing to do graffiti on the walls, but trying to be a real artist? That's hard."

"Graffiti is real art," Totz said. "You're amazing."

"I don't feel like it," Scoop said. "Everyone makes such a big deal about my art, but I feel like I'm faking it."

"Did anyone just hear that?" Slice said. "I've been hearing that *scritch, scritch, scritch* sound all night."

Totz shrugged. "I didn't hear anything."

"I heard it," Scoop said. "I thought it was Gleb and Lauren scrubbing dishes."

Just then, the cutest egg you ever saw came running over. She was out of breath, and her bow sat crooked on her head.

"Hey, Monella," Scoop said. "How are you?"

"Terrible," she panted. "I can't find Sal anywhere. We were supposed to meet for our daily speed walking around the Cafeteria, but he never showed up."

"Maybe he slept late," Slice suggested.

SAL IS OUR OTHER EGGY FRIEND!!!

"Sal never misses speed walking!" Monella cried out. "He was going to show me some new moves today. Plus, he was going to wear his new silver tracksuit. Something is wrong. You have to help me find him!"

Slice puffed out his cheesy chest. "Monella, we will find Sal for you," he said.

"Of course we will," Scoop said.

Monella sniffled. "Thank you," she said. "Thank you so much."

"Um . . . Um . . . Hi."

They all spun around to see a tiny piece of pasta peeking around the corner. He was short and was shaped like a tube.

Slice knelt down so he could hear the noodle's tiny voice.

"What can we do for you, little one?" Slice asked.

"Um . . . um . . . my name is Antonio. Glizzy and Sprinkles need to . . . um . . . see you. All of you. Um . . . they sent me."

Totz tucked away his notepad. "What's the trouble?" he asked.

Antonio looked at his feet, then looked at Slice, Scoop, and Totz. "Um . . . Scoop, someone . . . um . . . someone stole your art."

"My art?" Scoop said. "Which piece?"

"Um . . . um . . . all of it."

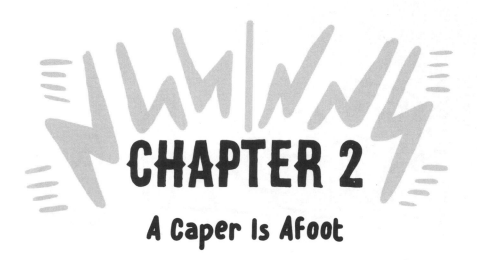

CHAPTER 2

A Caper Is Afoot

If there was ever any question of where Sprinkles was, you just had to follow the trail of, well, sprinkles. There was a clear, rainbow-colored path of them from the Cooler, between the legs of the Cafeteria tables, and right into the hallway.

Slice, Scoop, and Totz followed the trail of sprinkles.

"Hey, Scoop," Totz said to his ice-creamy friend.

"Don't you have to get back to the Freezer? This is the longest I've ever seen you without having to cool off."

Scoop looked puzzled. "I feel a cool breeze," she said. "It's stopping me from melting."

Slice looked around. "Could it be this?"

"The air-conditioning works again!" Scoop said, taking a deep breath. "As long as I stay near the vents, I can roam free. Now, let's find Glizzy and Sprinkles."

When they turned the corner, Sprinkles was slouched against the wall. Rainbow sprinkles poured from her eyes. Glizzy was patting her on the shoulder.

"I'm so sorry!" Sprinkles wailed. "It was my idea to hang all your beautiful, sparkly art out here for everyone to see, and now it's gone. It's all gone!"

Scoop rushed over. "I can always paint more," she said. "It's no big deal."

"It's a very big deal," Sprinkles said. "You trusted me, and I take that very seriously!"

"Really," Scoop said. "It's okay."

Glizzy stood tall and paced down the hallway. His tinfoil dragged behind him like a cape. "It's very strange," he said. "We only walked away for a few minutes to get more tape. We heard a strange sound, but by the time we got back here, all the paintings were gone."

Slice rubbed his cheesy chin. "What sort of sound did you hear?"

"It was a *scratch, scratch, scratch* sort of sound."

"No." Sprinkles sniffled. "It was more like a *scritch, scritch, scritch* sort of sound."

"Well, which sort of sound was it?" Totz asked. "Was it *scratch, scratch, scratch* or *scritch, scritch, scritch*?"

Glizzy thought about it. "Sprinkles may be right.

SCRITCH
SCRITCH
SCRITCH

It was more like *scritch, scritch, scritch*. But it's tough to say. We were busy looking for tape."

"What is the meaning of this?!? Why are you all in the hallway?"

It was Baron von Lineal, ruler of the Main Office. On either side of him stood his guards, two beefy staplers. Richard the dictionary loomed behind them.

"Is it wrong for us to be in the hallway?" Glizzy asked.

Baron von Lineal pointed straight at Glizzy. "It's wrong for you to be in the hallway when a caper is afoot."

"A CAPER IS AFOOT!" one of the staplers hollered.

"A caper is *not* a foot," Slice said. "A caper is a tiny pickled flower bud used in seasoning."

"I like capers," Scoop said. "They're very friendly."

"I do not mean the *food* capers," Baron von Lineal said. "I mean a caper as in a crime."

Richard the dictionary cleared his throat and spoke: "A caper is both a crime and a tiny pickled flower bud used in seasoning."

"Well, a crime is also not a *foot*," Slice said. "A foot is something you stand on."

Richard waddled closer. He towered over everyone. "*Afoot* means something is happening," he said.

"So, what you're saying is . . ." Slice tried to remember both definitions so he could put them together. "A crime . . . is happening?"

"Exactly," Baron von Lineal said.

"Exactly!" Totz repeated. "Someone stole Scoop's art."

WHO'S HE CALLING DRIPPY!!!

"I am not referring to the doodling of a drippy ice cream cone," Baron von Lineal said. "I am talking about something of much greater value. Something was stolen from the Main Office."

"What was stolen from the Main Office?" Glizzy asked.

"A cardboard box."

There was a long pause while everyone tried to figure out if Baron von Lineal was joking. But they all quickly remembered that Baron von Lineal had no sense of humor.

"A cardboard box has great value," Baron von Lineal explained. "It holds things. Art, on the other hand, does nothing. It hangs on the wall and collects dust."

"ART COLLECTS DUST!" one of the staplers announced.

"Now, wait just one second," Slice said, coming to Scoop's defense.

Scoop pushed past Slice. "We can argue about this later," she said. "People and things are going missing at Belching Walrus Elementary. My art is missing. A cardboard box is missing. Sal is missing. We need to catch the crook."

Just then, something scurried across the hallway

into the Auditorium. It was gray and fuzzy with a cottony white tail.

"What was that?" Sprinkles said.

But before anyone had a chance to answer, Slice, Scoop, and Totz ran into the Auditorium after it.

CHAPTER 3
The Chase Is On!

Now, I don't know if you've ever been on the floor of a dark auditorium chasing after a fuzzy critter with a cottony white tail before, but things can get out of hand fast. It is a maze of chair legs, chewed gum, shadows, and more chair legs that slopes ever downward toward the stage.

"Over here!" Slice shouted, darting to the left.

"No, something is moving over there!" Scoop cried out, pointing to the right.

"I'll guard the door!" Totz said. "If that critter can't get out, we've got them trapped."

But it was no use. Slice and Scoop searched every nook and cranny of the Auditorium. They went up and down every row of seats. They searched under the steps. They even looked in all the costume boxes.

There was no sign of a fuzzy critter with a cottony white tail anywhere.

Slice, Scoop, and Totz met by one of the air-conditioning vents so Scoop could cool off.

"That critter has to be somewhere," Totz said.

"Maybe it's better that the critter stays hidden," Slice said. "Remember what happened in the

Interdepartmental,   Interdisciplinary,   Intergalactic
Olympic Games when I had to race around the school?"

"A bird swooped down and tried to gobble you up,"
Totz said.

Scoop shivered. "The thought of that even gives *me*
the chills," she said.

THUNK!

Suddenly, the lights went on.

"Hello."

Slice, Scoop, and Totz spun around to see a bunny standing in the bright circle of a spotlight. She was gray with huge black eyes and floppy pink ears. Beside her stood a  brown-and-white hamster with pink toes, but this was no ordinary hamster. This hamster was the fuzziest furball you've ever seen. His mouth made a constant chewing motion.

"Awwww . . ." Scoop said.

Slice stepped forward and waved. "Greetings, my name is Slice," he said. "These are my friends Scoop and Totz. We come from a land called the Cafeteria."

"They call me Miss Bun-Bun," the bunny said. "This is my coworker, Houdini the hamster."

"Coworker?" Totz said. "What sort of jobs do you have?"

"We are Class Pets," Houdini the hamster said. "We act cute, eat pet food, and drink from upside-down water bottles."

Miss Bun-Bun nodded. "Not easy work, I'll tell you that."

"So, what are you doing here?" Totz asked suspiciously.

"We are . . . uh . . ." Houdini started.

"We are taking an evening stroll," Miss Bun-Bun said.

"Yes," Houdini said. "It gets cramped in our cages."

"Cages?" Slice asked. "We've never seen any cages."

"We live in the Science Room," Miss Bun-Bun said. "It is in the farthest reaches of Belching Walrus Elementary."

"Three hallways away," Houdini added.

Slice, Scoop, and Totz gasped. Three hallways away sounded very far.

"I've heard stories about the Science Room," Totz said. "They say no one who goes there ever returns."

Miss Bun-Bun and Houdini looked at each other and shrugged.

"It's just a room," Miss Bun-Bun said.

Scoop leaned against the air-conditioning vent. The cool breeze blew around her. "Have you been borrowing things from around the school?" she asked. "A cardboard

box, maybe? Some paintings? A little egg who happens to be our friend?"

Miss Bun-Bun walked across the stage. Her soft, padded feet were silent on the floor. "It's a bit rude to ask your new friends the very first time you meet them if they have been stealing," she said.

"Yes," Houdini agreed. "Maybe your little egg friend

is the one who stole the art and is living somewhere in the cardboard box like it's his own fancy apartment. Did you think about that?"

"We're sorry," Slice said. "We're just worried about Sal."

Houdini hopped onto a paint can and circled a few times before finding a place to sit. His pink feet were silent as well. "It's okay," he said.

"Now, if you'll excuse us," Miss Bun-Bun added, "it's late. We must get back to our cages."

"Of course," Totz said. "Have a good night."

As they walked out of the Auditorium and back toward the Cafeteria, Slice, Scoop, and Totz puzzled over who might be the real crook.

"You don't think Miss Bun-Bun could be right, do you?" Scoop said. "Sal couldn't have stolen the paintings and the box."

"An apartment sounds nice," Totz said.

"Nah," Slice said. "Sal would never miss speed walking, not for all the paintings and cardboard boxes in Belching Walrus Elementary."

"Plus, if Sal wanted a painting, I would just make one for him," Scoop said.

Totz scribbled some notes on his pad. "What about Miss Bun-Bun and Houdini?" he asked. "Do you think they lied to us?"

"Maybe," Scoop said. "But their feet were silent on the stage. It doesn't explain the *scritch, scritch, scritch* sounds we've been hearing. There's more to this caper than meets the foot."

The sound came from above, but there was nothing up there but the ceiling.

Just then, Monella came running up the hallway.

"She's been doing a lot of running today," Slice said.

"She's in good shape," Totz said.

"Monella," Scoop said. "What's going on?"

"Hurry," Monella said. "Other things have gone missing!"

CHAPTER 4
A Whole Tub of Hubbub

By the time Slice, Scoop, and Totz got back to the Cafeteria, a crowd had gathered. There was a load of food there. After all, where else was all that food going to hang out aside from the Cafeteria? There were a few other guests as well. And there was quite a *hubbub* going on.

Glizzy was making a stink.

Coach, the Head Whistle from the Gym, was tweeting as loud as he could.

François from the Art Room was painting a picture of how upset he was.

Even Baton, Conductor of the Music Room, was singing his own song.

Slice, Scoop, and Totz rushed over.

"What's all the hubbub about?" Slice asked.

"I'll tell you what all the hubbub is about!" Coach hollered. "Someone stole a jump rope from the Gym. I'm calling a foul!"

"Someone kidnapped Triangle from the Music Room!" Baton cried out. "This doesn't ring well with me."

"A Magic Marker haz been taken from ze Art Room!" François added. "Very off-color!"

Glizzy pushed through the crowd. "And someone snatched Red the apple from the Pantry," he said. "Whoever did this is rotten to the core."

The hubbub got more hubbubby. No one was happy about this.

Glizzy turned to Slice, Scoop, and Totz. "There was a day when I would have wrapped myself in a fresh piece of tinfoil and set out with  my friends Cheeseburger and Ice Pop to solve this mystery myself," he said. "But my bun is a little stale these

days and my friends are long gone—haven't seen them since the Great School Cookout. I'm not sure I could do all the legwork we will need to solve this mystery."

"Eet eez the greatest mystery ever to come to Belching Walrus Elementary," François said.

Slice looked around. Everyone looked scared. Slice was scared, too. His cheese felt bubbly. What if he was the next one to disappear? Or Scoop? Or Totz?

Slice knew they had to do something. "When we were in the Auditorium," he began to say, "we were talking to—"

He felt a sharp pain. Scoop had pinched his crust!

"What Slice *wanted* to say," Scoop said, "is that we were talking to *one another* in the Auditorium. We said how we would be happy to solve this mystery. Not only have things gone missing, but so have our friends."

Relief spread through the crowd.

"Triangle must be so worried, wherever she is!" cried Baton. "Oh, just ring out to me, Triangle. Ring out!"

"And Red the apple," Glizzy said. "He seems tough on the outside, but on the inside he's just a softie."

Totz pulled out his notepad and started jotting down notes. "I think everyone should go back to their rooms," he said.

"I agree," Scoop said. "Everyone will be safer in their rooms."

"That is a great play call." Coach whistled. "LET'S HUSTLE, EVERYONE!"

The crowd broke up.

Coach returned to the Gym.

François went back to the Art Room.

Baton walked off toward the Music Room.

And all the food headed back to the Pantry.

Glizzy climbed onto the counter and pressed the button for the intercom. "Attention, everyone at Belching Walrus Elementary. For your safety and the safety of others, we ask that everyone please return to their rooms as soon as possible. I repeat, please return to your rooms as soon as possible. We apologize for any inconvenience."

"Wow," Slice said. "He knows some long words."

"He's been around a long time," Totz said.

Glizzy called down from above. "Plus, I grew up reading food labels. My first word as a young frankfurter was *monosodium glutamate*."

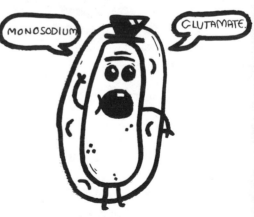

"I don't even want to know what that is," Scoop said.

"No," Glizzy said. "You don't."

Slice, Scoop, and Totz stood at the doorway and looked out at the hallway. The lights were dim. One of them flickered.

"I know we've been out there before," Slice said. "But somehow this seems like our most dangerous adventure yet."

Scoop nodded. "Creepy, scary, and weird all at the same time," she said. "Plus, I feel like someone is watching us."

Totz gulped.

"I think you may need some help," Glizzy said, hopping down off the counter and straightening his top hat.

"We can't ask you to come with us," Slice said. "Remember what happened last time?"

"Yeah," Totz said. "You got whomped pretty fiercely. We thought you were a goner."

"Oh, I won't be joining you," Glizzy said. "But there is someone you should meet."

CHAPTER 5
All the Kitchen Gadgets

Glizzy **led Slice, Scoop,** and Totz from the Cafeteria into the Pantry. He walked past a bucket and between the legs of a stool to the Cooler.

"What I'm about to show you is top secret," he said. "You cannot share this with anyone. Am I clear?"

Slice, Scoop, and Totz nodded.

Glizzy entered the Cooler and weaved through a maze of boxes and cartons.

Totz puffed out. "I can see my breath in here," he said.

"Yeah, it's a little cold," Slice said.

Scoop wiggled her cone. "I think it's just perfect," she said.

When they got to the very back of the Cooler, Glizzy pushed aside a package of frozen hamburger patties and knocked on the steel wall.

A muffled voice sounded from the other side. "What's the password?"

Glizzy looked around to make sure no one else was there. "Fettuccini Alfredo," he whispered.

There was a long pause. "That was last week's password," the voice said. "What is the *new* password?"

Glizzy glanced at Slice, Scoop, and Totz and smiled in embarrassment. "Um . . . chana masala?" he said, sounding unsure.

"Chana masala is a yummy Indian stew made with chickpeas," the voice said. "But that was the password *two* weeks ago."

A secret panel in the wall popped open, and the scent of salty deliciousness floated out. A slice of bacon stepped from the darkness. "What good is a password if people don't know it?" he asked.

"I thought that was the whole point of a password," Slice said. "So that people *don't* know it."

The slice of bacon looked at Slice, then at Glizzy. "Munching mulberries, who is this rude pile of cheese you've brought here?" he asked Glizzy. "He doesn't even know that passwords are for people in the know to know and for people not in the know to not know?"

TRY SAYING THAT 10 times FAST...

KNOW. I MEAN NO.

Glizzy introduced them. "Gang, this is my brilliant friend Rasher," he said. "Rasher, these are my friends Slice, Scoop, and Totz. They need your help."

Scoop's and Totz's hearts pounded at the delicious scent. They pushed past Slice and reached out to shake Rasher's hand. "Nice to meet you," they both said.

Rasher brushed them off and walked back to the secret door. "Yes, yes, everyone loves bacon," he said. "Please try to get over it and follow me before you all get freezer burn."

Scoop and Totz tripped over each other to follow Rasher while Slice and Glizzy trailed behind. The dark passageway twisted and turned.

"What is it about Rasher?" Slice asked Glizzy. "I can't help but like him."

"There is something about bacon people can't help but love," Glizzy said. "Everyone wants a piece of him. But for Rasher, it's a curse. He wants to do important work—work that will help all foodkind. Once, he invented a machine to keep food fresh longer.

"He invented a device to keep mice from nibbling at us."

Glizzy went on. "He even invented a vehicle that could leave Belching Walrus Elementary, a vehicle that would allow us to explore schools beyond Belching Walrus Elementary."

LEAPING LIMA BEANS! I CALL IT THE INVIGORATOR!

BURSTING BANANAS! I CALL IT THE DE-MICE-INATOR!

"Do you really think there are other schools out there?" Slice asked.

"But everyone just looks at him like a tasty morsel," Glizzy explained. "So, Rasher chose a life of hiding." Glizzy helped Slice under a metal bar. "Now, let's not fall behind."

By the time they caught up, they found themselves in a room lit only by a single light bulb. Pipes and wires criss-crossed in every direction. A long workbench stood against the wall. The room was cluttered with all sorts of tools and equipment. In the far corner stood something hidden under a large napkin. It seemed to shake and rumble.

Scoop and Totz had already told Rasher about the mystery at Belching Walrus Elementary. They had told him how Sal, Triangle, and Red were missing. They had told him how the cardboard box, the jump rope, and the Magic Marker were missing.

"... and whoever did all this stole my art, too!" Scoop said. "Twelve paintings in all."

"Prancing potatoes! A kidnapping, a robbery, *and* an art heist?!?" Rasher exclaimed. "We must solve this triple mystery right away."

Glizzy straightened his top hat. "These three want to do just that," he said, "but I believe they'll need a little help."

Rasher narrowed his eyes in thought. "I have just the things," he said.

Rasher started digging through boxes, rummaging through drawers, and digging through more boxes.

"He's so dreamy," Scoop whispered.

"I can't take my eyes off him," Totz said.

Finally, Rasher returned.

"First, you," Rasher said to Totz. "For you, I have made these..."

Rasher held out a pair of shoes.

"What are those?" Totz asked.

"Marching muffins! I call them sneakers," Rasher said.

"What do they do?" Totz asked.

"You put them on your feet," Rasher explained as he helped Totz slide his feet into them.

"Why would I want to do that?" Totz asked.

"Because when you push this button . . ." Rasher reached down and pressed the heel of the sneaker.

"Now you can skate anywhere," he said. "Super fast, super quiet."

Totz wobbled on his roller skates for a moment but then started to get the hang of it. Before long, he was doing clumsy circles and figure eights around the lab.

"This is going to take some practice," Totz said.

Rasher pushed the button on Totz's roller skate as he tottered past. The wheels folded up into the sneakers, and Totz fell down. "There is no time for practice," he said. "It is time for action."

Rasher turned to Scoop. "For you, I have this . . ."
He held forth a watch.

"Shuffling shallots! I call it a wristwatch!" he said.

"A wristwatch?" she said. "Every room in the school has a clock on the wall. Why do I need a wristwatch?"

Rasher smiled. "This is no ordinary wristwatch," he said, strapping the timepiece to Scoop's wrist. He pressed a button.

Beep, beep! Beep, beep! Beep, beep!

"It is a timer."

Scoop looked at Glizzy and Slice in confusion. Then back to Rasher. "Why do I need a timer?" she asked.

"Ask a six-minute egg who has been in the water for *seven and a half minutes*," Rasher said as though this would explain everything.

Scoop looked back at her friends. She didn't want to seem rude. "Thank you," she said. "Thank you very much."

"And for you," Rasher said, turning to Slice. "For you, I have something special."

Rasher pressed a button on his workbench, and a door slid open.

"Squealing squash! I call it a whisk!"

"A whisk?" Slice asked. "What does it do?"

Rasher grinned. "It will mix cream into whipped cream, smooth lumpy gravy, whip egg whites into foam, and mix hard-to-combine liquids with ease."

"Sounds dangerous," Totz said.

"One of the most dangerous weapons foodkind has ever seen," Rasher said.

"Thank you, Rasher," Glizzy said. "I'm sure these gadgets will come in handy for this triple mystery."

"So, Rasher," Slice said. "What's hiding under the napkin?"

"Yeah, it's shaking and rumbling," Totz said.

"That is top secret," Rasher said. "It is untested and unready. Now, forget about that and focus on your mystery."

Slice took hold of the whisk and held it up. "Our first stop is the Science Room," Slice said.

Rasher's eyes widened in terror. "Not the Science Room," he cried out. "Licking lollipops, not the Science Room."

CHAPTER 6
The Cafeteria Is Canvassing

So, what do we know so far?" Scoop asked as they walked out of the Cafeteria and back down the hallway.

"We know that no one from the Cafeteria has been to the Science Room in a very long time," Slice said with concern in his voice. "They say there are monsters living there."

Totz whipped out his notepad and read from it. "We also know that Sal, Triangle, and Red have been kidnapped. We know that a cardboard box, a jump rope, a marker, and your glittery art have been stolen."

"Why would someone want to steal all those things?" Scoop asked. "Do they have anything in common?"

They thought about it as they turned the corner and headed down the next hallway.

"I don't see any connection," Slice said.

"Me neither," Totz agreed.

"Then we must be missing something," Scoop said. "We either don't understand what the thief wants all that stuff for . . ."

"Or the thief isn't done stealing yet," Totz said. "We'd better canvass all the other rooms to see if anything else has gone missing."

"Canvas?" Slice said. "Isn't that what Scoop paints on to make her art?"

"No, *canvass*," Totz said. "With two *s*'s at the end. It means to go around and ask questions."

Slice moved the whisk to his other shoulder. "Okay, you could have just said that."

And that is exactly what Slice, Scoop, and Totz did. They went around and asked questions.

They canvassed the Gym.

They canvassed the Tech Room.

They canvassed the Main Office.

They canvassed the Art Room.

They canvassed the Music Room.

They canvassed the Library.

They even canvassed the cleaning supplies.

"So, things are still disappearing," Scoop said. "The plot thickens."

"If it gets too thick, I can use my whisk," Slice said.

"I've added all the missing things to my list," Totz said, tucking his notepad away. "I still don't see a pattern."

"Musical instruments and office supplies," Scoop said.

"Gym equipment and cleaning supplies," Slice added.

"Food, tech equipment, and art supplies," Totz said. "It doesn't add up."

They rounded another corner and headed down a long hallway. This one was extra dark. The lights were extra flickery. There were no cobwebs, but Slice, Scoop, and Totz felt extra creeped out, as though cobwebs were hanging all around them.

"The Science Room is over there," Scoop whispered.

As they headed down the hallway, Slice felt like someone (or something) was watching him. His cheese got a little melty.

Scoop stopped cold. "I hear voices."

Totz put a finger over his lips. They tiptoed down the hall and peered around the next corner.

The Science Room was dark and flickery (maybe even *more* than the hallway!) and lined with long black tables. Along the walls stood cage after cage, their doors wide-open. In the center of the room, a meeting was going on. They already knew Houdini the hamster and Miss Bun-Bun. But there was also a bunch of other animals they had never seen before. One had a shell on her back. Another was long and scaly with a skinny tongue that flicked out every few seconds. And two furry white mice huddled together. A fuzzy, yellow chick wearing a hat seemed to be running things.

"I believe we have everything we need to make our plan a success," the chick said, pacing up and down the row of animals. She gestured with her tiny wing at a white sheet that covered a small pile of objects.

"We just need one more thing, Napoleon," Houdini said. "The bait."

"Red the apple should be fine bait," Napoleon the chick said. She spun to face the mice. "Squeak? Whiskers? Where is Red?"

"Uh . . . he overpowered us," Squeak said timidly.

"We're very tiny," Whiskers added. "Red escaped."

"Do I have to do everything myself?" Napoleon asked.

"I wonder what's under that sheet," Slice whispered.

"Shh," Totz said. "They'll hear us."

Napoleon spun around and glared at the door. "WHO'S THERE?" she said.

"Um . . ." Slice tried to think of something to do. "Um . . . *Scritch, scritch . . . scritch?*" he said.

"It's jussst more soundsss from the air-conditioning ductsss," the snake hissed.

Slice, Scoop, and Totz breathed a sigh of relief.

Napoleon turned back to the meeting. "We will need new bait if this plan is to work." She grabbed the sheet and yanked it. The sheet flew off and revealed a cardboard box held up on one end by a Magic Marker. A jump rope was tied to the Magic Marker so when someone pulled it, the box would drop down.

Slice, Scoop, and Totz looked on in horror.

"We have to get out of here," Scoop whispered.

Slice and Totz nodded.

But when they turned around, they bumped into a glass fishbowl filled with water. Bulging eyes peered at them through the glass. "Where do you think you're going?" a fish asked. He was red with long, flowing fins.

"Who are you?" Scoop asked.

"My name is Finn," the fish said. "I am chief security officer for Napoleon the chick and the rest of the Science Room. What do you think you're doing?"

Slice looked at the fishbowl that had not been there a moment earlier. "How did you get here?" he asked.

"I patrol this hallway and all of the Science Room," Finn said, drifting side to side in his bowl. "There is nothing that escapes my ever-watching eyes."

Finn swam closer to the glass. His eye looked huge.

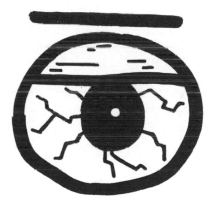

"No, I mean you're in a heavy glass fishbowl," Slice said. "How do you get around?"

"Never you mind that!" Finn said. "The more important question is what are *you* doing snooping around?"

"We're not snooping," Totz said.

"You're not?" Finn asked suspiciously.

"No," Totz said. "We're running!"

And with that, Slice, Scoop, and Totz ran.

CHAPTER 7
Racing About, Finding an Out

No wonder everyone is afraid of the Science Room," Slice said as they ran down the hallway. "They're monsters!"

"You said it," Scoop panted. "They want to catch more of us. Who knows what their evil plans are?!?"

Totz glanced over his shoulder. Napoleon was riding on Houdini, and the other animals followed.

They rounded a corner and ran past the Main Office.

"Lock your door!" Slice hollered to Baron von Lineal and the office supplies. "Don't let anyone in!"

The door to the Main Office slammed shut.

Farther down the hallway, they raced past the Library and the Music Room.

"Close your doors!" Scoop cried out. She had not been near the air-conditioning vent for a while and was starting to look drippy. "Emergency!"

The Library's and Music Room's doors slammed shut. Blinds over the Library's windows spun closed.

They rounded the next corner but ran straight into Napoleon, who was sitting on Houdini's back. All piled up like that, even a hat-wearing chick on a hamster looked scary.

"Where do you think you're running off to?" Napoleon chirped.

"We're running back that way," Slice said, spinning around.

They ran past the Gym, the Art Room, and the Tech Room.

"Close and lock your doors!" Totz cried out. "Code red!"

The doors to the Gym, the Art Room, and the Tech Room slammed shut.

They rounded the next corner and ran down the hallway.

"We are running in circles," Totz said. "There's the Main Office again!"

"Over here," Scoop said. She stopped by the air-conditioning vent.

"I know you're feeling drippy," Slice said, "but this is no time to cool off!"

"Help me lift it up," Scoop said. She grabbed the vent and started pulling. Slice and Totz knew what she had in mind. They worked their fingers between the slats and helped her.

The air-conditioning vent swung open, and they ran inside. Slice pulled it closed behind them, and they hid.

Within seconds, Napoleon galloped past on Houdini's back. "Seize them!" she chirped.

Other characters from the Science Room ran, hopped, creeped, scampered, or slithered past.

Slice, Scoop, and Totz sank to the floor to catch their breath and looked around. They were sitting in a narrow tunnel that reached off into the distance. The

walls, floor, and ceiling gleamed silver. Here and there, other tunnels branched off in different directions—left and right, even up and down.

Scoop breathed in the cool air. Her melty drips went away.

"Where are we?" Totz asked. His voice echoed a little.

"We are in the air-conditioning ducts," Scoop said. "These tunnels bring cool air everywhere."

"It's super clean, but it's also super creepy," Totz said.

Slice knocked on the wall of the duct. It made a hollow sound. "Do you think we could get back to the Cafeteria through them?"

"There's only one way to find out," Scoop said.

They looked at one another.

"I'm not so sure about this," Totz said. "Maybe we should go back out to

SCRITCH SCRITCH SCRITCH SCRITCH

the hallway. The Cafeteria is only around the corner and down the hall."

"No way," Slice said. "Those evil animals are everywhere."

Slice, Scoop, and Totz looked out through the vent. A giant red eye was peering back at them.

"Aah!" they screamed. "FINN THE FISH, CHIEF SECURITY OFFICER OF THE SCIENCE ROOM!"

They ran down the silver duct.

"How does Finn get around in that bowl?!?" Slice said as they made a few quick turns.

"No time to worry about that," Scoop said. "Let's find the Cafeteria."

Scritch, scritch, scritch!

The sound was getting louder.

"That way!" Totz said, pointing away from the sound. They bolted down another silver hallway.

They made a few more quick turns and stopped.

"We can't just keep running," Slice said, out of breath. "Let's figure out where we are."

"How do we do that?" Totz said. "It's not like there are any signs around here."

Scoop leaned against the wall. "First, we have to figure out where we are," she said. "Then we can figure out where we need to go."

"So, how do we figure out where we are?" Slice asked.

"Easy," Scoop said. She walked down the duct and

peered through the nearest air-conditioning vent. Slice and Totz joined her.

"It smells like grouchy books," Slice said. "We must be in the Library."

"That's not nice," Scoop said.

"Okay," Slice said. "I saw all the shelves filled with books. I see Spex Bifocals and Richard the dictionary, too."

"So, if we're in the Library now . . ." Scoop said.

Totz looked both ways down the silver duct. "We have to go that way," he said, pointing.

They walked slowly down the tunnel until they reached the next vent. They peered through to see Baton and dozens of instruments pacing around nervously.

"See?" Totz said, "We're at the Music Room. That's closer to the Cafeteria than the Library."

"That must mean we're headed in the right direction," Slice said. "Keep going."

"Maybe we should keep going a little faster," Scoop said.

They rushed along the silver duct and made a left turn at the end. The tunnel headed up like a ramp.

"Sliiiice . . . Scooop. . . . Totzzzzz . . ." the voice said again.

They glanced back to see a dark shape coming toward them.

"Sliiiice . . . Scooop. . . . Totzzzzz . . ."

They ran up the ramp.

They made two more turns and came to a dead end. There was a vent. They pushed.

"It's stuck!" Scoop said.

"Push harder," Slice grunted.

The dark shape was coming closer. They could hear its footsteps on the metal floor.

"It's moaning and groaning!" Totz cried. "All the scariest monsters moan and groan."

Slice stopped pushing and looked at Totz. "How many scary monsters do you know, and how many of them moan and groan?" he asked.

"Not now," Totz said. "Keep pushing!"

Thoom! Scrape . . . Thoom! Scrape . . . Thoom! Scrape . . .

They pushed with all their might. The dark shape was making its way up the ramp. The moaning and groaning grew louder.

One corner of the vent popped loose.

Thoom! Scrape . . . Thoom! Scrape . . . Thoom! Scrape . . .

"Push . . . harder . . . !" Scoop grunted.

They pushed harder.

The other corner of the vent popped loose, and the vent swung open.

Scoop was the first one through. "Jump!" she cried out.

She leaped from the vent into the Cafeteria. Slice and Totz followed.

THUMP . . .

They landed on a carton. It broke their fall.

Glizzy came running over, followed closely by Sprinkles and several pieces of penne.

"Hurry!" Slice panted. "There's a monster . . ."

"It's chasing us!" Totz added.

OW...

But before anyone could do anything, the vent popped open again and the dark shape fell out. It rolled over on its back.

It was Red the apple.

A big chunk had been bitten out of him.

CHAPTER 8

If Life Gives You Apples...

Red," Slice said, kneeling down to help him. "What happened?"

"I was walking along, minding my own business, when someone put me in a paper bag," Red said. "It was so dark . . . so crinkly . . ."

"That sounds terrible," Scoop said.

Red went on. "I was taken to the Science Room,

where they held me in a cage while they made their evil plans."

"A cage . . . ?" Sprinkles cried. "The horror!"

"But I escaped." Red coughed. "No cage can hold Red the apple." He coughed again.

"Did you bend the bars and muscle your way out?" Antonio the penne asked.

"No," Red said. "I reached out and opened the latch. That creepy fish was guarding the door, so I found my way into the silver tunnels."

"The air-conditioning ducts," Totz said.

Red nodded and coughed again. "I was trying to find my way back here when someone . . . no . . . some-*thing* took a bite out of me."

"What was it?" Totz asked.

"It all happened so quickly. I—I don't know," Red said. "Now, please, I need to rest."

Glizzy knelt down to inspect Red's injury. "I've seen this before," he said. "The bite will soon turn brown. Then his shiny red skin will start to wrinkle. If we don't act fast, Red will spoil."

Sprinkles burst into tears. Rainbow sprinkles fell to the floor.

"What do we need to do?" Slice said. "I'll give my cheese, my pep-peroni, anything."

"There is only one thing that can save him now," Glizzy said. He helped Red to his feet. "Come with me."

And with that, Glizzy, Red, and the penne pastas disappeared into the Pantry.

"Oh dear," Sprinkles said. "What do you think they will do with poor Red?"

"All we can do now is hope," Totz said.

Slice rose to his feet. Determination burned in his eyes. "We have to put an end to this," he said. "Those Class Pets can't get away with what they did."

"You heard what Red told us," Totz said. "It wasn't the Class Pets at all. It was a monster in the air-conditioning ducts."

"If they hadn't apple-napped him, none of this would ever have happened," Slice said.

"And if this can happen to Red, it can happen to any of us," Scoop said.

Slice turned to Totz. "What do we know so far?" he asked.

Totz took out his notepad. "I have my list of all the things that went missing . . ."

MISSING PEOPLE:
SAL THE EGG
TRIANGLE THE TRIANGLE
RED THE APPLE
COACH THE WHISTLE
SNIP THE SCISSORS
CHIME THE BELL
12 paper CLIPS
MISSING THINGS:
SCOOP'S ART.
CARDBOARD BOX
JUMP ROPE, MARKER
WIRES, WIRE BRUSH.
GLITTER

"But some of that stuff has turned up," Scoop pointed out. "The Class Pets were using it to make their trap."

Totz crossed the cardboard box, marker, jump rope, and Red off the list.

"So, what does the rest have in common?" Scoop said. "Why would the Class Pets want all that stuff?"

They thought about it for a moment more. Slice scratched his crust.

"I don't see a pattern," Totz said.

Scoop looked toward the hallway. "There's only one way to find out," she said.

"You can't go back out there," Sprinkles said. "You saw what they did to Red."

"We can't live in fear," Slice said. "The Class Pets are new here, and we have to straighten this out."

"The sooner the better," Totz said.

Slice, Scoop, and Totz set out right away. They headed down the hallway, made their first right, and then turned left at the Library. Before going any farther, they paused at an air-conditioning vent so Scoop could cool off.

"Why is it always the three of us who have to save the day?" Scoop asked.

"Well, there was that one time when Nanner, Spoon, and Salty saved the day," Slice said.

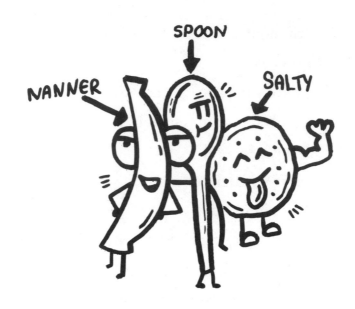

NANNER SPOON SALTY

"Poor Salty," Totz said. "He was so crisp and filled with fiber."

"And then there was Sammy, Juice Box, and Nugz," Slice said.

"None of them ever returned," Totz said. "They went off to that well-balanced meal in the sky."

"So, uh . . . Totz," Slice said. "Any chance you have a poem that might get us a little pumped for this?"

SAMMY

JUICE BOX

NUGZ

"Yeah," Scoop said. "I could use some lyrical courage."

Totz flipped through his notepad and narrowed his eyes. "Nothing that really fits this situation," he said.

"Maybe you could make something up?" Slice said.

Totz thought for a moment and started.

"We were hanging in the Pantry with all our pals
When Monella stopped down. She was looking for Sal.
Scoop's art went missing and so did a box.
A jump rope, a marker, everything but my socks.
We met a few critters, they seemed nice at the time,
Little did we know they committed a crime.
They're making a trap. They even messed up poor Red.
Now we're goin' to the Science Room to put this to bed."

"How do you do that?" Slice asked.

"Yeah," Scoop said. "So good."

"It needs a lot of work," Totz said, looking down at his sneakers. "You ready to go?"

"My chocolate, vanilla, and strawberry scoops are nice and cool," Scoop said.

They marched past the Main Office and down the

hallway toward the classrooms. The hallway was darker and flickerier than ever.

"HALT!" It was Finn the fish, who was in his bowl at the doorway to the Science Room.

"Calm your gills," Slice said to Finn. "We just want to talk."

"You may not enter," Finn said. "We are on high security alert."

Scoop jostled Finn's bowl. His water sloshed around. "And what will you do if we don't listen to you?" she said.

"I'll . . . I'll . . ." Finn thought about it a moment. "I'll write you a citation!"

"Ooh, that's pretty scary," Totz said. "A citation?"

"You don't want a citation from me," Finn warned. "My citations are—"

Slice stepped closer. "Actually, Finn, I *do* want a citation from you. Go ahead. Write me a citation."

A CITATION IS AN OFFICIAL ORDER TO APPEAR IN COURT.

IT'S A TICKET.

Finn looked at them. "Well, one of you will have to write it for me," he said. "It's too wet in my bowl to write anything."

Slice, Scoop, and Totz walked past Finn into the Science Room.

The rest of the Class Pets were huddled around the trap they had built.

As usual, Napoleon was talking. "We need to find more bait!" she chirped.

"Aha!" Scoop said. "So, you *are* trying to catch us and eat us!"

The Class Pets spun around.

"You're going to pay for what you did to Red," Slice said. "This is not the way we treat one another at Belching Walrus Elementary."

Miss Bun-Bun hopped a few hops closer. "You

don't understand," she said to them. "We're not trying to eat you."

"You're not?" Totz said.

"But you're sneaking around," Scoop said. "You're building traps and trying to lure in the rest of us using our friend Red as bait."

"Applesss are not good for sssnakes," Slither said. "Neither are pizzzza, iccce cream, or tater totsss. They upsssset our tummiesss."

"Then what's this fancy trap for?" Scoop asked.

"And why do you need one of us to be bait?" Slice asked.

Houdini walked closer. "We're trying to catch one of our own," he explained. "Daisy the ferret escaped, and she won't come back."

CHAPTER 9
Out of the Frying Pan . . .

The Class Pets gathered around Slice, Scoop, and Totz.

"You know . . ." Napoleon said. She paced back and forth and glanced at the trap, which was still set up in the corner. "Three tasty morsels like yourselves could help us."

"We agree," Squeak and Whiskers both said at the same time. "Tasty morsels are useful."

"Useful in their tastiness," Shelly the turtle said slowly.

"We're not going to be bait for your trap," Scoop said. "You're just going to have to find some other way to catch Daisy."

"The air-conditioning ducts are a huge network of tunnels," Napoleon said. "Much of it is unexplored and dangerous. The only way to find Daisy is to lure her out here."

"With food," said Finn, who had mysteriously appeared behind them.

"Why do you need to find her so badly?" Scoop asked.

"Yeah, if she wants to live in the air-conditioning ducts, just let her," Totz said.

Napoleon shook her head. "I'm afraid it's not that simple," she said. "Long ago, there were Class Pets at Belching Walrus Elementary. Shelly is the only one left from those old days. She told us the stories."

They all looked at Shelly, who crept forward slowly.

"It is true," Shelly said slowly. "There used to be pets of all sorts in this school. We lived in peace and happiness in every classroom, in every grade. Cages and tanks of all shapes and sizes. Everything was perfect."

"That sounds amazing," Totz said. "What happened?"

Shelly looked off into the distance. "Escape is what happened," she said. "There was a gerbil named Virgil

who thought he was better than all this. He didn't like his life in a cage. He didn't like the crunchy pet food they put in his bowl every day. Virgil decided to seek something better. He wanted a life of adventure."

"Good for Virgil," Slice said.

"Bad for Virgil," Shelly said slowly, glaring. "Bad for every animal on two, four, or zero legs at Belching Walrus Elementary. Days after Virgil's escape, things began to change around here. Cages were tied shut. Bricks sat atop fish tank lids. We were trapped like prisoners. Before long, cages at the school began to disappear. They were getting rid of us."

"That's terrible," Scoop said.

"Yes . . ." Shelly said slowly. "Terrible and serious and all very real. I am the only one left from those old days, mostly because I move very slowly, I eat the lettuce they give me, and turtles live a very long time."

Napoleon cleared her throat. "We are worried that if we don't find Daisy, we will disappear, too."

"I've never heard of a rabbit disappearing before," Miss Bun-Bun said. "I'm scared."

The Class Pets gathered around. "You have to help us," Squeak and Whiskers said together. Their eyes looked as large as saucers. "Please?"

"Why us?" Totz asked.

"It's obvious," Napoleon said. "You have a whisk."

I FEEL VERY THREATENED RIGHT NOW...

They looked at Slice's whisk.

"Are you going to tell me to bop Daisy on the nose with it?" Slice asked. "That would be mean."

"Of course not," Napoleon said. "It's shiny. Daisy loves shiny things."

"Yeah," Houdini said. "Haven't you noticed? Everything Daisy steals is shiny and sparkly."

"Daisy sure does love shiny and sparkly things," Squeak and Whiskers said.

Totz whipped out his notepad and had a look.

MISSING PEOPLE:
SAL THE EGG
TRIANGLE THE TRIANGLE
~~RED THE APPLE~~
COACH THE WHISTLE
SNIP THE SCISSORS
CHIME THE BELL
12 PAPER CLIPS

MISSING THINGS:
SCOOP'S ART
~~CARDBOARD BOX~~
~~JUMP ROPE, MARKER~~
WIRES
WIRE BRUSH
GLITTER

"Triangle, Coach, and wires," Totz said. "All shiny and sparkly."

"Snip, wire brush, and Chime," Slice said. "Same."

"My glittery art and twelve paper clips," Scoop said. "All of it is shiny and sparkly."

"But what about Sal?" Slice asked. "Eggs aren't shiny."

"They're not sparkly, either," Totz added.

"Oh, I hope Sal is okay," Scoop said. "We have to save him!"

Slice held up his whisk. "Scoop . . . Totz . . ." he said. "It looks like we have a job to do."

Miss Bun-Bun and Houdini opened the air-conditioning vent, and Shelly stood underneath it so Slice, Scoop, and Totz could climb in.

"One more thhhing," Slither said. "Sssqueak and Whiskersss have been working on a map."

Squeak and Whiskers brought out a piece of paper and showed it to them.

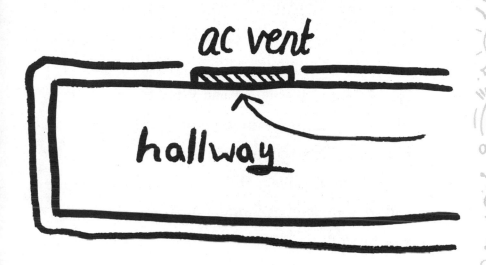

"It's as much as we were able to figure out," Squeak and Whiskers said. "But it's very accurate."

"Remember," Napoleon said, "you have to bring Daisy here so she can get back in her cage."

"Just follow the *scritch, scritch, scritch* sounds," Squeak and Whiskers said.

"She really is lovely when you get to know her," Shelly said slowly.

"How will we find our way out?" Totz asked, pulling himself into the shiny duct. "It's like a maze in here and every vent looks the same."

"You've got a map," Squeak and Whiskers said at once.

Before they could say anything more, the Class Pets closed the vent. Slice, Scoop, and Totz followed the shiny duct. Just like before, every twist, every turn looked the same, and soon they were completely lost.

"Stay behind me," Slice said. His voice quavered in fear. "I've got the whisk."

HELLO...

Scoop ran her hand along the wall. "Look at this," she said. "Claw marks."

"And over here," Totz whispered. He knelt to the floor. "Glitter everywhere."

SCRITCH SCRITCH SCRITCH SCRITCH

"It looks like there was a struggle," Slice said.

Something scurried behind them. When they spun around, it was gone.

Totz gulped. "Slice . . . Scoop . . . I think we may have gone out of the frying pan . . ."

CHAPTER 10

Into the Fryer

. . . And into the Fryer," Totz said.

They continued down the duct. They made a left and two rights. The duct went up and then down.

Slice stopped. "I hear something," he whispered.

They all listened and heard a tiny voice. *"Left, right, left, right, left, right . . ."*

"What is that?" Scoop asked.

"Left, right, left, right, left, right . . ."

"There's only one way to find out," Slice said. They turned the next corner to find a large shiny room filled with shiny items. They saw metal wire brushes, Scoop's glittery art, bundles of sparkly wire, and all the folks who were missing from their rooms. They saw Triangle the triangle, Coach the whistle, Chime the silver bell, Snip the scissors, and twelve paper clips tied up with string.

On top of it all sat a long, furry creature with spindly whiskers and razor-sharp claws. She shivered, and her beady eyes darted left and right. Her head perked up, and she hissed. Then she lay down and closed her eyes.

Slice, Scoop, and Totz shrank back.

"What do we do?" Scoop whispered. "The Class Pets said Daisy was nice, but she looks . . ."

"She looks a little off," Totz said.

"I'd say," Slice said. "She tied up our friends and is holding them prisoner."

Deep in the farthest corner, they heard the same voice: *"Left, right, left, right, left, right . . ."*

"And what about that voice?" Scoop said. "Is someone trying to give us directions in this maze of tunnels?"

"I don't think so," Totz said, peeking around the corner at Daisy. "What kind of directions is '*left, right, left, right*' over and over again?"

"What if we lured Daisy away?" Scoop suggested. "Then we could check it out."

"How would we do that?" Slice asked, leaning on his whisk.

Scoop held up her wrist and disappeared down the passage. "Just *watch* . . ." Slice and Totz hid in the shadows until they heard a beeping sound.

Beep, beep . . . beep, beep . . . beep, beep . . .

Daisy lifted her head. "Beepsies," she said.

Beep, beep . . . beep, beep . . . beep, beep . . .

Daisy's furry ears perked up. "I likes beepsies more than shinies."

Beep, beep . . . beep, beep . . . beep, beep . . .

Within moments, Daisy arose and darted down a

hallway, her long, noodly body twisting wherever her paws took her.

Scritch, scritch, scritch!

"We'd better get in there," Slice said. "Who knows how long Scoop will keep Daisy busy?"

Slice and Totz rushed into the room.

"Hey, y'all," Slice said. "We're here to save you."

"My heroes!" Chime rang out.

Slice untied Snip, who began snipping through everyone else's strings.

"We need to hustle!" Coach hollered. "That slinky furball is a few bowling pins short of a full rack."

Beep, beep . . . beep, beep . . . beep, beep . . .

"Has anyone seen Sal?" Totz asked.

No one answered. Slice and Totz glanced at each other with worry.

"Help me!" It was Scoop.

"Scoop's in trouble," Totz said to Slice. "We'd better go."

Slice turned to Coach. "Can you lead this crew out of here?" he asked.

"They don't call me Coach for nothing," he said with a grin. "Now, go help your teammate."

Slice and Scoop raced off and followed the sound of the beeping. They made a few turns and found themselves looking down a long silver hallway.

They heard the sound of claws on steel ducts: *scritch, scritch, scritch!*

They heard the sound of a timer beeping: *Beep, beep . . . beep, beep . . . beep, beep!*

They still heard the echoing voice: *"Left, right, left, right, left, right."*

Then they heard Scoop: *"Aaaaaaaah!"*

Suddenly, Scoop ran across the hallway from one duct to another. Seconds later, Daisy scampered across the hallway in a different direction.

Slice and Totz snapped into action.

"Bop her with your whisk!" Totz said as they ran down the hall.

"No way," Slice said. "I still think it's mean."

They made a left and tried to follow Scoop, but the tunnel split in so many directions they couldn't find her.

Beep, beep . . . beep, beep . . . beep, beep!
Scritch, scritch, scritch!
"Aaaaaaaah!"

"Listen for the sound of the beeps," Totz said. "That way!"

Slice and Totz ran in the opposite direction, stopping every few seconds to listen for the beeping.

Finally, they rounded a turn to see Scoop backed into a corner. She had a claw mark down her vanilla scoop. Daisy was standing over her. "Forget about shinies!" she hissed. "I wants the beepsies!"

Scoop spotted Slice and Totz. She took off her watch and tossed it to them.

Totz caught it. "I've got this," he said to Slice. He pressed the button on his sneakers, and the wheels popped out.

Beep, beep . . . beep, beep . . . beep, beep!

Daisy turned and started after Totz. "Beepsies! Beepsies!" she snarled. "I wants the beepsies!"

"In case I don't make it," he said to Slice, "I want

you to take my notepad. There's a poem I've been working on and—"

Slice gave Totz a shove down the hallway. "No chance," he said. "You can show it to me when Daisy is back in her cage. Now, get going!"

Totz grinned. He turned around and skated away. *Beep, beep . . . beep, beep . . . beep, beep!*

Slice dove aside just in time. Daisy barreled past. "Beepsies! Beepsies!" she said.

Slice rushed over to Scoop. "Are you okay?" he asked.

"Fine," she said, standing up. "Not even a crack in my cone."

"But your vanilla scoop . . ." Slice said.

"What, this?" Scoop asked. She wiped her hand over her vanilla scoop and smoothed the ice cream. The claw marks were gone. "Let's get going. Totz needs our help."

CHAPTER 11

Roller Tot

Totz was not an expert skater at all. He wobbled and had trouble turning (especially turning left!), but with a crazed ferret chasing him, he figured out how to go fast quickly. He zipped up one duct and down another. He went up one ramp and down another. All the time the watch beeped in his hand.

He had no idea which way to go, so he just kept skating. He made another left, and then he made a right. He zipped past Slice and Scoop.

"Just keep skating," Slice said. "We'll figure something out!"

But there was no time to just keep skating. Totz's legs were getting tired, and he was huffing and puffing. He had never worked this hard before. And the more tired he became, the closer Daisy got.

Beep, beep . . . beep, beep . . . beep, beep!

He made a right, and then he made a left. He leaped over a tunnel that went straight down.

"Wait," he said. "What's that smell?"

Totz paused a split second to sniff. He smelled the aroma of bacon.

"No one can resist bacon," he said.

Totz tried to follow the smell. He made a few more turns until he got to an older part of the tunnels, darker with less shine.

Beep, beep . . . beep, beep . . . beep, beep!

He skated as hard as he could. An air-conditioning vent was up ahead!

"Only one chance," Totz said.

He skated down the hallway, leaped into the air, and smashed into the vent.

"Jumping juice boxes!" Rasher yelled as Totz landed on the floor of the laboratory. "What's the password?!?"

"Beef Wellington . . . Cheese fondue . . . I don't know . . ." Totz threw himself into Rasher's arms and panted. "You . . . have to . . . help us . . . !"

Within seconds, Daisy burst into the lab. "Beepsies! Beepsies!" she hissed.

Slice and Scoop tumbled out of the vent just after her.

Rasher lifted Totz to his feet. "Come with me," he said.

The two raced across the lab while Daisy looked wildly about and Rasher pulled the napkin off his top secret project. It looked like an oatmeal box with wheels made of cookies. Wires and tubes looped out of holes in the box and disappeared into other holes.

"I call it the Snack-Mobile!" Rasher said. "It runs on soda and mints!"

Totz climbed in as Rasher shoved a few mints into the back. The car began to shudder. Bubbles started foaming out of the hood.

Beep, beep . . . beep, beep . . . beep, beep!

Daisy hissed and leaped at them. At the last second, Slice landed on Daisy. She spun around and swiped at Slice's cheesy chest. Slice dodged Daisy's claw and

rolled off her back, but it gave Rasher and Totz just enough time to get the Snack-Mobile started.

"Go, go, go!" Scoop cried out, jumping into the car. Slice dove into the car crust-first. His feet stuck up into the air.

Rasher stomped on the Soda Pedal. The cookie wheels began to spin, and the Snack-Mobile launched from the lab, foam spraying from the back.

"But we'll never make it out of that tiny tunnel," Totz said.

Rasher pressed a button, and a large door swung open on the far side of the room. They could see the Pantry. In fact, this door led out from under the utility sink, right where Slice, Scoop, and Totz liked to chill out.

The Snack-Mobile blasted through the Pantry into the Cafeteria, with Daisy right behind them.

"To the Science Room!" Scoop cried out, ducking Daisy's claw.

They made a left and blasted out into the hallway. Daisy was never more than a step behind. "Beepsies! Beepsies!" she hissed.

They drove past all the rooms in the school, the Snack-Mobile constantly spraying foam behind them. Doors began to open. They saw Coach and all the sports equipment from the Gym. They saw François and all the art supplies from the Art Room. They saw Chip and the gear from the Tech Room. They saw Baton and all the instruments from the Music Room. Spex Bifocals popped her head out of the Library with Richard the dictionary. Even Baron von Lineal came out of the Main Office with the office supplies.

They skidded around the next turn, but the Snack-Mobile started sputtering.

"Put more mints in the chamber!" Rasher called to Slice.

Slice looked around. "Are you sure there are more mints? I can't find them anywhere."

Rasher shook his head. "I knew I forgot something."

They made another turn, but the Snack-Mobile was losing speed.

"Go down that hallway," Totz said.

They rolled past the Main Office but came to a stop.

Rasher stomped on the pedal, but nothing happened. No bubbles. No foam.

Rasher turned to Slice, Scoop, and Totz. "You'll have to finish this one on your own," he said.

"But how will we do it without you?" Scoop asked.

"You'll find a way," Rasher said. "Now, go!"

Slice, Scoop, and Totz bolted down the hallway toward the Science Room just as Daisy rounded the corner.

Beep, beep . . . beep, beep . . . beep, beep!

Daisy ran faster.

"Give me the watch," Totz said. "I can skate faster."

He pressed the button on his sneakers.

Nothing happened.

"I forgot to mention," Rasher called from the Snack-Mobile, "my roller skate sneakers only work a few times."

"Beepsies! Beepsies!" Daisy hissed.

Totz looked at Slice and Scoop in worry.

"Tell the other tater tots to stay crispy," he said.

And with that, Totz ran off.

CHAPTER 12

The Crispiest of the Crispy

Totz ran down the hallway into the Science Room.
All the Class Pets were there.

"Halt or I'll give you a citation!" Finn said.

Totz rushed past him, took the beeping watch, and
tossed it as hard as he could. Napoleon caught it.

Daisy darted into the room and started toward Napoleon, her claws scraping on the cold tile.

"Beepsies! Beepsies!" she growled.

Beep, beep . . . beep, beep . . . beep, beep!

"It's a crazy game of keep-away with a crazed ferret!" Scoop said.

Napoleon tossed the watch to Miss Bun-Bun, who immediately threw it to Houdini. Napoleon to Miss Bun-Bun to Houdini to Slither to Shelly to Squeak and Whiskers to Finn.

SPLOOSH!

The watch dropped right into Finn's bowl.

The beeping stopped.

"Uh-oh," Napoleon quacked.

Daisy lifted her head. She calmed down a little. "No more beepsies," she said. "Back to the tunnels. Back to my shinies."

"Not if I have something to say about it."

It was Sal. He was wearing his shiny silver tracksuit.

"That's why Daisy kidnapped Sal," Scoop said. "She didn't want *him*. She wanted his *tracksuit*."

Sal leaped from the air-conditioning vent and darted toward Daisy's open cage.

"Forget speed walking," he said. "Time to run. Left, right, left, right, left, right!"

He dove into the cage. Daisy leaped after him.

As quickly as he could, Sal took off his tracksuit and threw it into the far corner.

Daisy darted past Sal, grabbed the shiny tracksuit, and started backing out of the cage.

"Hurry," Miss Bun-Bun said. "She's getting away!"

"Somebody do something!" Houdini cried.

Bop!

GO ON.....

It was the tiniest *bop* (really, it was more of a light push), but it was enough to keep Daisy in her cage. Sal slipped past her, and Scoop swung the door shut. Just in time, Totz pushed the lock into place.

FERRETS CAN SLEEP UP TO 20 HOURS A DAY!!!

Daisy took the tracksuit and curled up in the darkest corner of her cage. "Shiny . . . Shiny . . ." she said as she drifted off to sleep.

"She really does like it in her cage," Napoleon said.

"She feels very safe there," Miss Bun-Bun added. "She sleeps nearly all night and day."

The Class Pets cheered.

"You've saved us all," Napoleon said. "How can we ever repay you?"

"We'll need to make sure Coach, Triangle, Snip, Chime, and all twelve paper clips are okay," Scoop said.

Totz nodded. "We also need help returning every shiny object to their owners," he said.

"Of course," Ms. Bun-Bun said. "But is there anything else?"

"Anything," Houdini said. "Just ask."

Rasher limped into the room. Although he was missing a few bacon bits, he still looked as tasty as ever. "The Snack-Mobile is destroyed," he said.

Slice, Scoop, and Totz glanced at one another.

"There is one thing you could do for us," Slice said.

When they returned to the Cafeteria, almost everyone in the school was there to greet them. And they did what we all know the citizens of Belching Walrus Elementary were so good at.

And they did.

The End.

"Wait a second," Scoop said. "This is *not* the end. There are so many loose ends to tie up."

"Life is full of loose ends," Glizzy said. "Not everything has a tidy wrap-up."

"But what happened to Red the apple?" Totz asked.

"Yeah," Slice said. "Is he okay?"

"I'm fine."

They all spun around. The crowd parted.

Red the applesauce hobbled forward. "After Daisy bit me, they couldn't save my skin," he said. "They couldn't save my seeds."

Slice, Scoop, and Totz rushed over.

"I'm so sorry, Red," Scoop said. "We should have come sooner."

"It's okay," Red said. "I feel better than ever. So loose. So juicy."

"But . . . the cane . . ." Totz said.

"Oh, this?" Red said. He twirled the cane around, tossed it into the air, and caught it. "I just like how it looks. It's my new style."

Slice held his whisk in the air. "You know what this party needs?"

"What does it need?" Glizzy said.

"This party needs a song." Slice looked at Totz. He looked at Scoop, Sal, and Monella.

Totz flipped through his notepad. "I have just the thing."

Scoop smiled. "Me too."

Sal and Monella nodded. "Me three and four," they said.

Totz pulled out his banjo and tuned it. He started playing a loop of quick banjo twangs.

Scoop hung her paintings on the walls behind them. The art sparkled like a thousand twinkling stars.

Sal and Monella turned over a pot and started banging out a beat with wooden spoons.

Before long, Totz started to sing.

"Chillin' with my pals, hanging under the sink,
When we hear about someone kicking up a big stink.
All kinds of stuff missing, missing here, missing there,
Art, boxes, rope, even Sal's underwear.

Glizzy and Sprinkles sent us on a great quest,
Didn't wanna do it, but we had to acquiesce.
Deep in the Auditorium, it felt like a maze.
It only took minutes, but it felt like ten days.

Houdini and Bun-Bun didn't tell us the truth,
So, we set out to find not the half, but whole proof.
Rasher gave us gadgets to help us, no lie.
Skates, whisk, beeper—we felt like real spies.
The chick and Class Pets were hatchin' a plan,
They had to catch Daisy to save their whole clan.
They built a big trap. The bait was poor Red.
But their plan was more rotten than six loaves of moldy
  bread.
Me and my buddies agreed to help out.
Into the ducts, we needed to
  scout.

Lo and behold, what did we see?
Triangle, Coach, Snip, my
  grandma's TV.

We thought it would be easy.
The ducts were oh so breezy,
But running makes me queasy.

AND HE SMELLS IRRESISTIBLE.

Slice, he is so cheesy.
When we finally found Daisy,
We ran so fast it drove us crazy
The memories are hazy,
But I know we weren't lazy.

Through the ducts, through the
school, Daisy was chasing,
Fangs, claws, hissing—real trouble
we were facing.
Rasher came through with a box
and some wheels,
With mints and some soda, we
had the Snack-Mobile.

We tore through the hallways, blasting out that foam.
Daisy didn't know it, but she needed to get home.
Slice bopped her in like pushing grapefruit . . .
And the ferret curled up with Sal's silver tracksuit."

BRING IT HOME, TOTZ!

Now, for those of you who are familiar with the legendary Totz of Belching Walrus Elementary, you know that sometimes he bursts into song. And you probably know that Scoop, Sal, and Monella have helped him with his shows before. However, this song, this particular song about their adventures with the Class Pets, drove everyone bananas.

Everyone cheered louder than ever.

Everyone clapped harder than ever.

Everyone danced more dancier than ever.

"No citations for anyone!" Finn called out.

Everyone looked at Finn. Slice walked around him and inspected him closely.

"How do you get around?" Slice said.

"Who cares?" Glizzy said. "Let's just have fun!"

And they did.

The End (really).

Missed what happened in the second Bad Food adventure? Turn the page and find out!

CHAPTER 1
Where We Begin All Over Again

It was an average night at Belching Walrus Elementary. The doors were locked, the hallways were quiet, and the moon and stars shone brightly through the high windows. Oh, and also all the food in the Cafeteria was jamming out.

No, what I meant to say is that the food in the Cafeteria at

HEY MAN!!

Belching Walrus Elementary actually comes alive each night to party. Every night.

And ever since the folks from the other rooms in the school helped stop Baron von Lineal's evil plans ...

Okay, what I meant to say is ever since the folks from the other rooms at Belching Walrus Elementary helped stop Baron von Lineal's *misguided* plans, they've been coming to the Cafeteria each night to hang out as well.

And, as always, our favorite foodie friends—Slice (a brave slice of pizza), Scoop (a triple scoop ice cream cone—vanilla, chocolate, AND strawberry), and Totz (a crunchy, delicious, and trendy tater tot)—were doing their own thing under the utility sink.

Of course, their new friends came around often to say "Wassup."

Before we go on too long, it might be a good idea to meet some of our new friends. After all, if you

don't like these new friends, you might decide to put this book down and do something completely differ-

ent. Maybe you'd prefer to swim in a pool filled with chocolate pudding? Or drink a big glass of warm prune juice? Maybe you'd rather be buried under a pile of chubby, yapping puppies? So, here goes...